PROMISES

Ch@t
by Barbara Catchpole
Illustrated by Georgina Fearns
Published by Ransom Publishing Ltd.
Unit 7, Brocklands Farm, West Meon, Hampshire GU32 1JN, UK
www.ransom.co.uk

ISBN   978 178591 253 5
First published in 2016

Barbara Catchpole

How it started

Chatboy1: It's OK! It's OK! This is private! They can't see us – or what we say! Calm down, *Lonelygirl*.

Lonelygirl: I don't get it! Who were all those

people? Why were they talking to me like that? Gross!

CB: When you log on with a name like **Lonelygirl**, you are saying to all the guys … well, that you want to … Well, people aren't nice, you know. So not cool! IDGI either really!

LG: I'm not stupid! I can look after myself! I've just never been in a chatroom before!

CB: Didn't look like it, *Lonelygirl*. Admit it! I just rescued you!

Chatrooms are not cool!

LG: I just want to chat to someone. You know, I've nobody to talk to. My mum's always busy and my sister hates me. Everybody hates me! I'm a bit lonely, so I thought …

CB: Sure, but just use this. We are alone together here, if you see what I mean.

LG: Just …

CB: Yeah?

LG: Who the hell are you?

CB: Er ... just a boy.

LG: Not sure I can talk to a boy properly, but I guess you'll do. Never really had a chat with a boy before. I didn't know they could chat. Let's see – first question: are you a nutter?

CB: I'm an alien with ten hairy arms.

LG: That would actually be OK, 'cos I am an alien with ten hairy legs.

CB: You can push me on a trolley thing!

LG: OK, but I'll have to use my purple tentacles!

LG: Mum's yelling! Gotta go! Same time/room tomorrow?

CB: Sure – *no* – got football. Hour later!

LG: Football! With no legs! Bet you suck!

CB: Yeah the rules are sorta rubbish for

us ten-armed aliens. Goalie's gr8
though!

Red hair, alien
eyes and spit

LG: You're late!

CB: Had to smuggle the tablet up
here. KPC! My little brother Joe
wanted to play Minecraft. I've

locked him out. He's kicking the
door.

LG: *KPC?*

CB: Keep Parents Clueless!

LG: I can't do that stuff!

CB: Me neither – learning it though!
Do you type with your feet?

LG: ?

CB: Ten legs.

LG: LOL! See I'm trying!

CB: Let's get to know each other a bit. Let's start basic – I am a boy alien. Bit of a computer geek – but I've not got spots or glasses.

LG: Hair?

CB: Yes, I've got hair. You?

LG: Yes but it's red – really red, not ginger. I wanted to put a deeper red on it but, of course, Mum won't let me. My sister, Lacey, told her it wasn't allowed. Lots of the girls do it – the teachers can't tell if you do it bit by bit. Sophie at school puts blue on hers – you can see.

CB: I like red hair. Is it long?

LG: It goes down to my ten feet. OK, Mr Not Bald – what's your hair like?

CB: Sweaty – just got back from football – just brown and in my eyes at the front. Brown eyes – all seven of them!

LG: LOLA! Gotta go and do my Maths homework. Old Spratton goes ballistic if you don't hand it in – spits and everything.

CB: Tomorrow?

LG: Sure ... I'd like that.

Sushi v Big Macs

CB: Hard core getting to know each other. Favourite food?

LG: Sushi. It looks so neat – tiny little parcels. Mum gets it from Marks and Sparks. You?

CB: I'm not eating raw fish just because it's wrapped up nice. You're such a girl! Big Mac and chips – enough calories to feed Sheffield. Favourite colour?

LG: Blue.

CB: Red – a good friend of mine has red hair! Star sign?

LG: Not sure about all this – Mum says I'm not to give real info about myself online.

CB: She's dead right there, but even Sherlock couldn't track you down on the basis of liking sushi and your star sign.

LG: OK – Leo.

CB: Leo who?

LG: It's a star sign, divvy!

CB: I knew that!

LG: Gotta go – bloomin' Joe wants to play bloomin' Minecraft.

Secrets

LG: What it is – I just can't seem to
make friends. I got to this school
late and everyone was like, paired
up. There are some girls who
really get at me too because of

the red hair thing. They post
things on FB.

I can't tell Mum – she's got
enough to do, now Dad's gone.
I'm just so lonely. I just wanted to
talk to someone. Some days I got
so I couldn't stop crying. I felt like
going out to the park and just
running, running away.

CB are you there? Are you there?
Talk to me! I'm sorry! Is this too
heavy? Say something!

CB: I'm here! I'm not going anywhere.

I'm just not good at this stuff. We've got each other now – don't freak out – things are going to get better. DO NOT run away – that is really, really, really dumb and difficult and dangerous and – yes – DUMB! Keep yourself safe!

LG: Are you calling me dumb?

CB: Running away!

LG: Would you miss me?

CB: Yeah.

CB: Where would I find another ten-legged alien?

CB: Hey, LG, where is your dad?

LG: Is it OK if I don't say?

CB: Sure.

So normal
we're weird

LG: What about you? What's your family like?

CB: Oh, I've got both parents at home. Dad's a dentist. Mum's a dental nurse, so we're alright for teeth!

LG: Do they talk about teeth at
dinnertime?

CB: Yeah, but you get used to it. And
I've got Mattie, my little brother.
He's just seven so that's a pain,
but I guess maybe they were too
interested in teeth ...

LG: Hard to believe!

CB: Maybe they saw me and
thought: this child is so perfect,
we don't need any more!

LG: Yeah, right!

CB: Anyway – we're so normal, we're weird!

LG: That must be nice …

Introducing the sister from hell

CB: You're late.

LG: Lacey stole my tablet to do her stupid college stuff.

CB: Brain surgeon?

LG: Nail technician.

CB: More useful every day – for a girl, I mean. Little birds on your nails and stuff. I don't know what I'm talking about!

LG: Yeah – even if I needed brain surgery and she was the only person in the universe who knew anything about it, I'd still ask her to do my nails.

Own goal

CB: I've had a really rubbish day.

LG: Whassup?

CB: Finally got picked for football.

Only the second team – but still, never played before against another school. I was really hyped. And I scored a goal.

LG: That's cool! What's the problem?

CB: It was for the other side. Just sort of bobbled off my boot as I was trying to keep it out. The rest of the team were OK about it, but I won't get picked again. I feel like … well …

LG: You need a hug.

CB: I do.

LG: Hug, hug, huggedy, hug!

LG: CB?

CB: Yes?

LG: Is 'bobbled' a real word?

Why we should get tough with axolotls

LG: I loathe axolotls!

CB: OK …

LG: You know what they are, right?

CB: Lizard things?

LG: I think so … They should be salamanders but they never grow up. They just loll about the tank looking gross, like they're cookie dough. They have to be kept warm and fed certain things and they never grow up and go out to work and do grown-up salamander stuff. You never get rid of them! They just lie there like giant white slugs! They won't grow up and leave!

CB: One: I'm sure it's normal to hate

aquatic animals. Two: boy, you really hate your sister, don't you?

LG: You are too clever, CB! My nan says you can be so sharp you cut yourself.

Budgies and guinea pigs

LG: I like budgies though. My nan's got one that says: *Why don't you shut your beak?*

CB: I like guinea pigs. They look like

they're kind and when you stroke them it sounds like their motor is running.

LG: And they do neat little poos …

CB: I like the ginger ones. They're always tougher than the rest and they have cute little circles in their fur.

LG: I like you.

CB: I like you too.

Super Powers

LG: What is your Super Power?

CB: I play piano up to Level Geek.

LG: Wow! Awesome!

CB: Not very cool though – you can't take a piano to a beach party. What's yours?

LG: Stuffing things up.

CB: You just don't know what it is yet. It could be that you're clever, or it could be that you're funny. I think it's one of those. Although with all those tentacles, it could be opening loads of cans at once.

LG: That would be a rubbish Super Power. *Can Girl.*

CB: I'm just imagining the costume …

LG: It would have a giant baked bean on the front …

Are you my boyfriend? Please!

LG: My sister asked if I have a boyfriend.

CB: What did you say?

LG: Well, you are a boy and you are my friend …

CB: OK.

LG: Don't sound too happy about it!

CB: I meant, 'yes please'.

LG: Now you sound like you are asking for more chips at dinner time!

CB: Mmmmmmm … chips …

Meeting up IRL

LG: Spratton went ballistic today. We had a Maths test and the boy next to me did nothing but draw things on his paper.

CB: Things?

LG: Rude boy things that I am not going to talk about.

CB: Gotya.

LG: So Spratton yelled and there was real hard-core spitting over the front row. A spit-storm – they needed waterproofs. Spitcoats.

CB: Yeah my brother's mate says Spratton can really spit – like those dinosaurs in Jurassic Park.

LG: Wait a minute … Spratton. You're local! We could meet up! Why didn't you say?

CB: I just didn't want …

LG: To meet up?

CB: To spoil it.

LG: Where are you? Tell me now!

CB: One of the dead and alive villages just out of town.

LG: I am so excited! That is amazing!

How about 11.00 Saturday
morning in the coffee bar at the
bus station?

CB: Are you sure? LG – you really
don't know that I am not a crazy.
You should not be doing this! And
… and … it will change things.

LG: No it won't! It won't! Promise you'll
be there?

CB: I promise.

LG: Awesome!

Busted!

Lacey (yelling):

> Are you mad? Are you crazy?
>
> You are out of your tiny
>
> looney-tunes brain, little sis!
>
> Completely out of your gourd!

Lonelygirl (yelling):

You're spying on me! You're
reading my private stuff! You
sneaking, cheating, spying,
lying ... Get off me!

Lacey:

You need a good slap! And
you're meeting him! Have you
no sense at all? He is an axe
murderer or at least a
twenty-stone, fifty-year-old
sweaty lorry driver in a string
vest!

Bonkers! Sheer madness!

Lonelygirl:

He's not, he's lovely!

Lacey:

I'm telling Mum because it is just crazy!

Lonelygirl:

No, Lacey, please. *Please!*

Lacey:

Yes I am – or you'll be dead and Mum will be crying on TV and it will be my fault. I'll have to do one of those sad 'this is what happened' things for television.

I *have* to tell her, Gina. You must
see that, little sis!

Lonelygirl:

I hate you and I'm never talking
to you again.

Lacey:

Suits me! And by the way ...

Lonelygirl:

Yes?

Lacey:

You've got snot on your face!

Calling
social services ...

Mum:

You are **not** going, Gina May

Peters.

Lonelygirl:

I **am** going. You can't stop me!

Mum:

Actually I *can* stop you, young lady. You are just fifteen and I am not going to let you meet a strange man in a café.

If I have to call social services or involve the police through your Uncle Jake, I will do it. I am not having you lying dead in a ditch somewhere.

Lonelygirl:

Ditch? There aren't any ditches. We live in Sheffield.

Mum:

It's what people say.

Lonelygirl:

I hate you. He's just a boy. If
I don't turn up, he'll think I've
stood him up. I'm the only
person he can talk to.

Mum:

And he's the only person you
can talk to?

Lonelygirl:

Yes.

Mum:

> The only person in the world? So
> not the person who has loved
> you since you were a baby? No!
> Some boy on the internet ...

Lonelygirl:

> Yes. He gets me!

Mum:

> That is how they trap you, you
> silly girl. They pretend they are
> fifteen when they are really thirty
> or forty or a hundred and eighty
> years old, with wrinkles and a
> walking stick.

They are very clever. They get
you to meet up, put something
in your drink ... and ... and ...
I can't even think about it!

Listen to me. Gina. I love you.
Please listen to me! It is so
dangerous! It will be some dirty
old perv!

Lonelygirl:

You think so?

Mum:

I think so, darling.

Lonelygirl:

> Mum,will you come with me?
>
> I'm scared, but I have to know.

Mum:

> I'll come with you, but we'll
>
> have Uncle Jake on speed dial.
>
> We'll take Lacey. Even an axe
>
> murderer would be scared of
>
> her! Ah, come here, lovey, let
>
> me hold you, don't cry!

Nearly there ...

Lonelygirl: Nearly at café.

With my mum. What is going to

happen?

Chatboy1: In café already. Sitting at back.

I can't tell her what is happening! This is just horrible! My whole family watching us!

The café 1

Lonelygirl

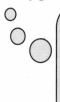

There he is! Sitting at the back! Twenty stone, fifty and wearing a leather jacket with egg stains down the front.

Lonelygirl

Oh look – he's just dropping some more down his front. And … nice burp! The whole café must have heard that! I think I am going to cry. This is the worst feeling ever. Mum was right, Lacey was right. *Lacey was right!* How can I live with that? She is going to be so in my face about this! I am such an idiot! How could anyone like me? I should have known! OMG! He's getting up and walking straight towards us with a big grin on his face. Nice black teeth … what a horrible sweaty smell.

The café II

Lonelygirl

Walking straight towards us and straight out the door. Now he has moved I can see Chatboy1 sitting reading the menu. With his glasses (what a lying liar). And OMG! With his mum and his dad! And his little brother! His whole family! She's nudging him and pointing at us. She must have found out too! And he's looking up at me. He's pointing at his mum and pulling a face and doing that twirly thing with his finger to say 'she's mad'. I'm pointing at my mum. Not mad – they just care about us! He's pointing at my bright red hair and giving me a thumbs up.

He has the loveliest smile ever ... I feel like I really know him. I think everything's going to be OK ... more than OK ...

Oh he's getting up ... he's holding out his hand ... I'm touching him!

The café III

Chatboy1

Wow! Lonelygirl is gorgeous!

MORE GREAT READS
IN THE PROMISES SERIES

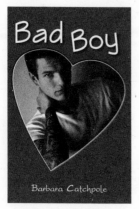

Bad Boy

by Barbara Catchpole

Taylor has had some disastrous boyfriends. There was the smelly computer geek who wrote code all day, and there was the one who was football mad and only wore Liverpool shirts.

Then Taylor meets Josh. He is tall, hunky and drop-dead gorgeous. It's perfect! Or is it?

Picture Him

by Jo Cotterill

Aliya loves taking photos. She talks with a stammer, but who needs words when you have pictures?

But when Aliya looks at her latest series of photos ('zombie princess', taken with her friend Zoe) she sees a murky figure in the background of many of them. Is she being stalked?